LOOK AND FIND

Disney's
ATLANTIS
THE LOST EMPIRE

Illustrated by Art Mawhinney

Cover Illustrated by Sue DiCicco

Written by Lynne Suesse

Published by
Louis Weber, C.E.O.
Publications International, Ltd.
7373 North Cicero Avenue
Lincolnwood, Illinois 60712

www.pubint.com

Manufactured in U.S.A.

8 7 6 5 4 3 2 1

ISBN 0-7853-5185-X

PUBLICATIONS INTERNATIONAL, LTD.

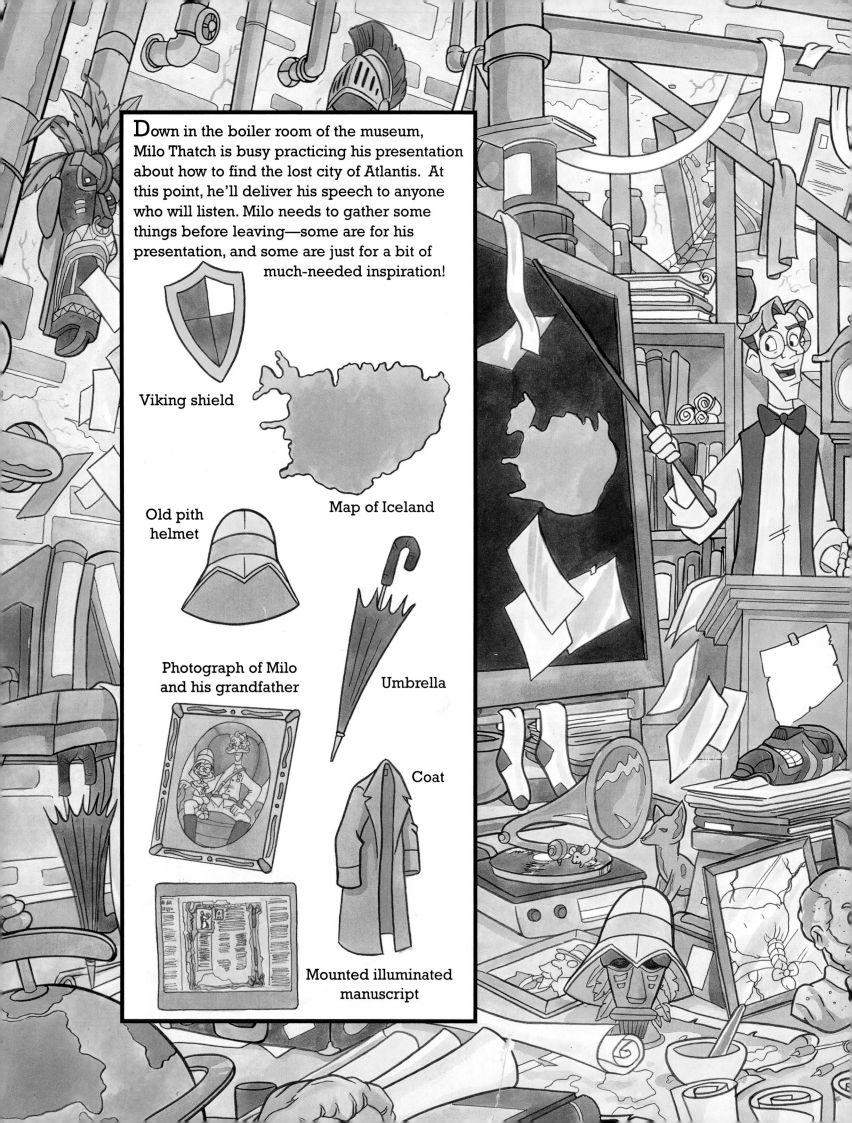

Down in the boiler room of the museum, Milo Thatch is busy practicing his presentation about how to find the lost city of Atlantis. At this point, he'll deliver his speech to anyone who will listen. Milo needs to gather some things before leaving—some are for his presentation, and some are just for a bit of much-needed inspiration!

Viking shield

Map of Iceland

Old pith helmet

Photograph of Milo and his grandfather

Umbrella

Coat

Mounted illuminated manuscript

Mild-mannered Milo Thatch has great ideas, but the big wigs at the museum won't listen to him! Nobody wants to hear Milo's story about *The Shepherd's Journal*, a book that explains where Atlantis can be found underneath the ocean. Help Milo find the members of the museum board before they scatter!

Harcourt

Fonebone

Freenbean

Potzrebie

Kaputnik

Trousdale

Wise

Hahn

Helga brings Milo to Preston Whitmore's artifact-filled mansion. Whitmore, an old friend of Milo's grandfather, not only promises to fund an expedition to find Atlantis—he also has the long-lost *Shepherd's Journal*! Help Milo search through this scene to find these other valuable pieces in Whitmore's collection.

Cleopatra's headdress

Shakespeare's tights

Ben Franklin's kite

Napoleon's boots

De Soto's map collection

Socrates' thinking cap

Mozart's greatest hits

Betsy Ross' sewing kit

Milo is finally going on an expedition to find the lost city of Atlantis! When Milo sees the enormous ship being loaded with supplies and equipment, he is astounded. Look around the loading bay to find these crew members as they prepare for their great adventure.

Mole

Cookie

Mrs. Packard

Rourke

Helga

Vinny

Sweet

Audrey

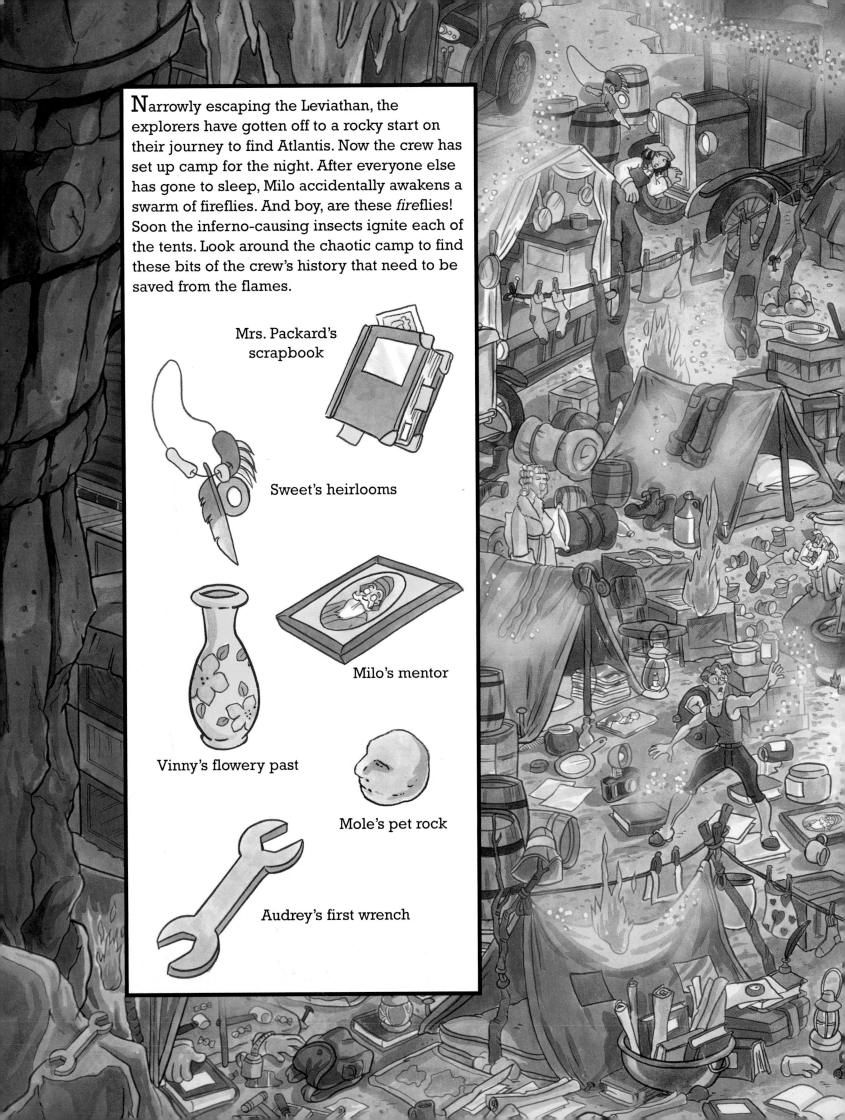

Narrowly escaping the Leviathan, the explorers have gotten off to a rocky start on their journey to find Atlantis. Now the crew has set up camp for the night. After everyone else has gone to sleep, Milo accidentally awakens a swarm of fireflies. And boy, are these *fire*flies! Soon the inferno-causing insects ignite each of the tents. Look around the chaotic camp to find these bits of the crew's history that need to be saved from the flames.

Mrs. Packard's scrapbook

Sweet's heirlooms

Milo's mentor

Vinny's flowery past

Mole's pet rock

Audrey's first wrench

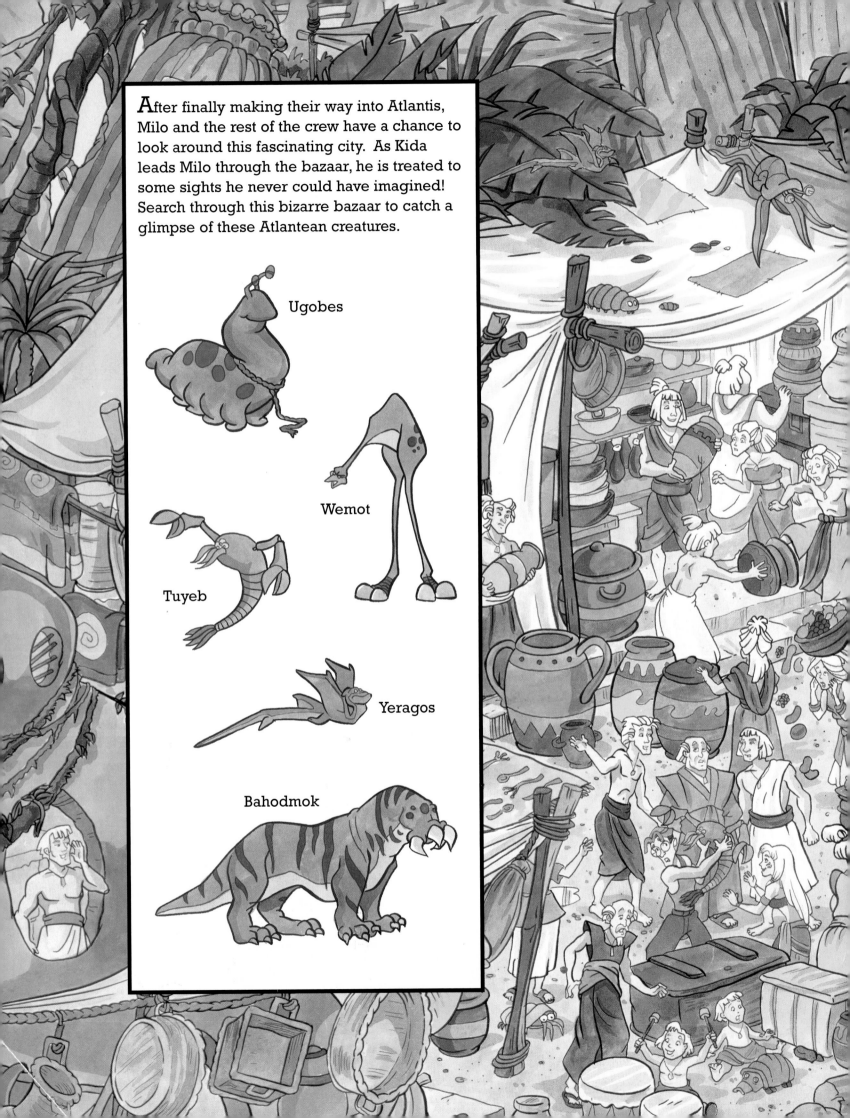

After finally making their way into Atlantis, Milo and the rest of the crew have a chance to look around this fascinating city. As Kida leads Milo through the bazaar, he is treated to some sights he never could have imagined! Search through this bizarre bazaar to catch a glimpse of these Atlantean creatures.

Ugobes

Wemot

Tuyeb

Yeragos

Bahodmok

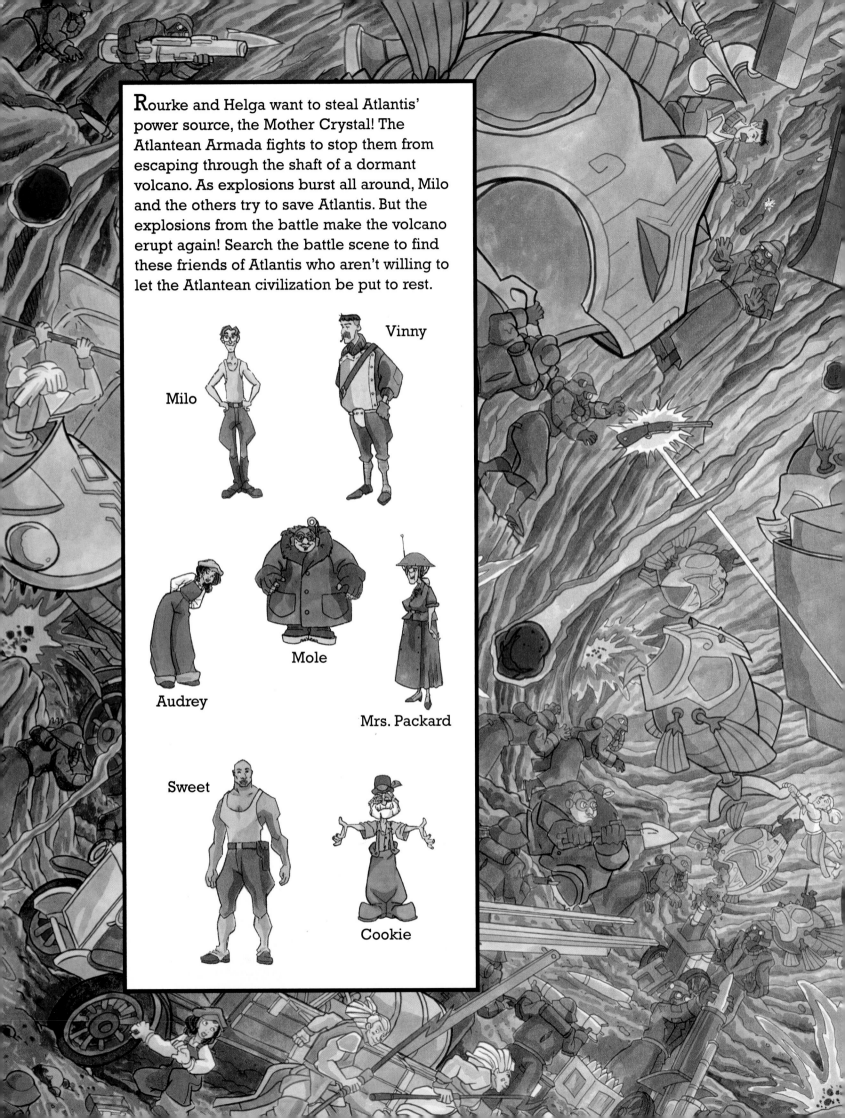

Rourke and Helga want to steal Atlantis' power source, the Mother Crystal! The Atlantean Armada fights to stop them from escaping through the shaft of a dormant volcano. As explosions burst all around, Milo and the others try to save Atlantis. But the explosions from the battle make the volcano erupt again! Search the battle scene to find these friends of Atlantis who aren't willing to let the Atlantean civilization be put to rest.

Milo

Vinny

Audrey

Mole

Mrs. Packard

Sweet

Cookie

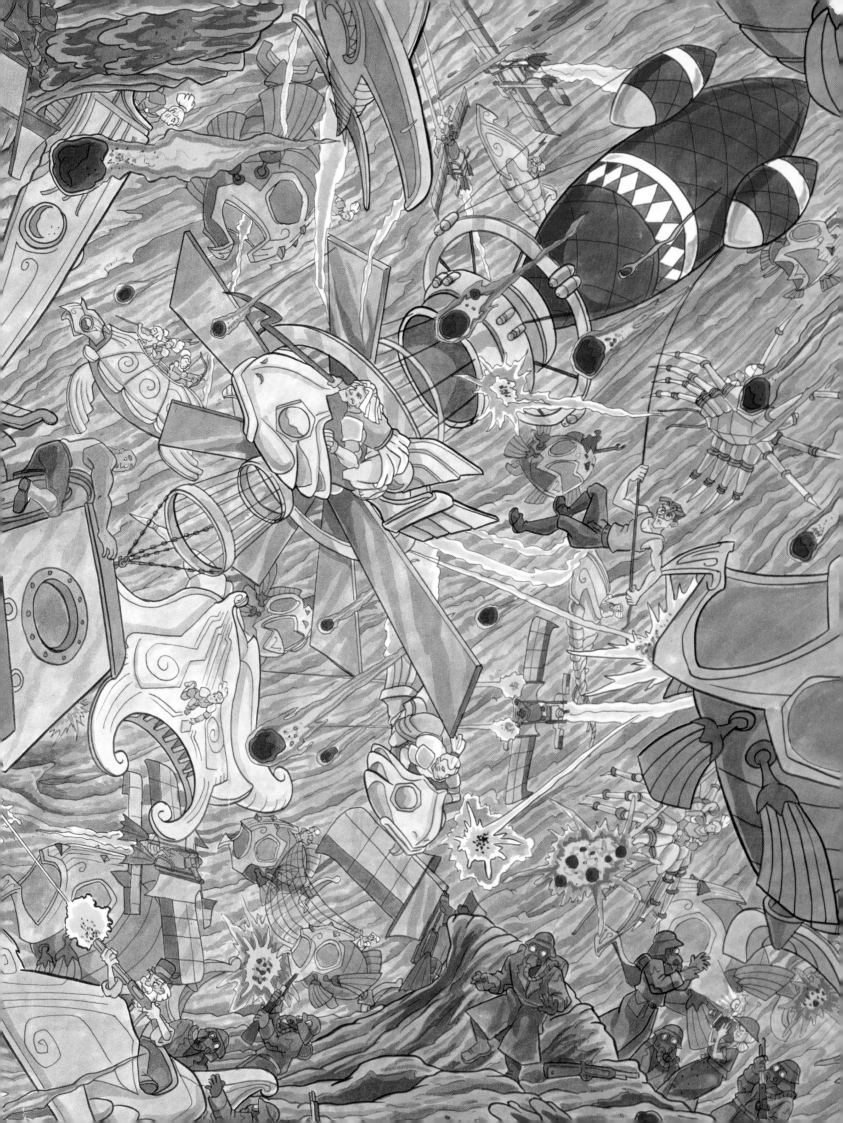

The Shepherd's Journal has survived through the centuries and provided the map to Atlantis. Milo journeyed very far to find the lost city, but the Journal has traveled much, much farther! Trace the Journal's journey through time and history by moving through this time line. Discover the identities of the Journal's keepers by decoding their names, which have been written here in Atlantean. Use the key in the back of the book to help you.

THE ATLANTEAN ALPHABET

Milo studied long and hard to learn the Atlantean language. You can learn to read and write Atlantean too! The language is written in such a way that it reads left to right, and then right to left, in alternating lines. For example:

Atlantis is a lost population
deep under the ocean

would read:

Atlantis is a lost population
naeco eht rednu peed

a b c d e f g h i j k l m

n o p q r s t u v w x y z

ch sh th

— · : ⋮ ·| | |· |: |: ✝
0 1 2 3 4 5 6 7 8 9

Use this key to decode the names of more hidden items throughout the book.

The boiler room sure is cluttered!
In addition to old artifacts,
Milo has left a few personal items lying around.
Can you find them?

Everyone in the museum is trying to avoid Milo.
Some of the board members are even trying to hide or run away, with a little help from these items.

Whitmore has collected tons of souvenirs and trinkets over the years.
These are some of his favorites.

Find these things the crew will definitely
need for its long sea voyage.

The fireflies have turned the campsite into a blazing mess.
Without getting burned, search for these items.

The city of Atlantis is different from any place on earth.
Explore the bazaar to find these uniquely Atlantean things.

Find these items without getting hit by flying lava
as Milo and friends battle for Atlantis.

The Shepherd's Journal has journeyed far.
See if you can locate these semi-historical items from its past.